To my super-patient, grocery-shopping husband, Bob,
my two wonderful daughters, Rayelle and Devon,
my artistic granddaughter, Samantha, and my
mother-in-law, Helen, who always knew I could do it

Who Wants Broccoli?
Copyright © 2015 by Val Jones
All rights reserved. Manufactured in China.

ISBN 978-0-06-230351-6

The artist used watercolor and a whisker of colored pencil
to create the illustrations for this book.

Typography by Rachel Zegar
15 16 17 18 19   SCP   10 9 8 7 6 5 4 3 2 1
❖
First Edition

Who Wants BROCCOLI?

By Val Jones

HARPER

An Imprint of HarperCollinsPublishers

A hodgepodge of pets lived at Beezley's Animal Shelter.

There were hamsters,

and guinea pigs,

parrots

and bunnies,

kittens

and turtles, and . . .

Broccoli!

Broccoli had lived at Beezley's Animal Shelter
for almost his whole life.

Early each morning, Mrs. Beezley brushed and fluffed all the animals.

When she finished, Mrs. Beezley would say, "There's a lid for every pot and a pot for every lid."

Then she opened the shelter for business.

All day, every day, Broccoli watched as
people came in to pick out their perfect pet.

Broccoli loved to show everyone how high
he could toss his bowl into the air . . .

and catch it every time.

He would show them how fast he could run
by chasing his tail around and around.
Then he would show off his great big . . .

BARK!

He barked when the desk dinger dingled.
He barked when the doorbells tinkled.
He barked when the telephone jingled.
Everyone covered their ears when the big barker let loose.

One day, while Broccoli watched out his window,
a big truck rolled up.

A boy named Oscar and his mom were
moving into the house across the street.

Mom had promised Oscar he could adopt
a pet as soon as they were settled in.

Oscar imagined how much fun it would be to
play in his new yard with a big, fun dog. . . .
Broccoli imagined how much fun it would be
to play in a yard with a boy!

Broccoli was so excited. He jumped his biggest jump, barked his biggest bark, then picked up his bowl filled with water and tossed it as high as he could. He soaked everybody in the shelter.

Mr. Beezley mopped and mumbled, "This noisy, messy pot will never find a lid."

Then Mr. Beezley pushed Broccoli's cage into the storeroom, where he couldn't cause any more trouble.

Without anyone to see his tricks,
Broccoli slid his bowl off his head.

Then he sat quietly,
completely ignoring his tail.

When he heard the desk dinger dingle, Broccoli rolled his eyes.
When the doorbells tinkled, he circled once, then lay down.
And when the telephone jingled, he just poked his nose out of
the cage and snortled.

The next Saturday morning, Oscar and his mom
headed to Beezley's Animal Shelter.

Oscar was sure he heard barking just the other
day and could not wait to pick out his perfect pet.

Mrs. Beezley told Oscar's mom that all the
animals in the shelter were very well behaved.

Bird Watching
Your house or mine
Call 321-555-2213

"How about a sweet, soft bunny?"

"Or a cute, furry hamster?"

"Or an adorable kitten?"

"Or maybe a clever turtle?"

Oscar slowly shook his head.

Mom said, "Maybe we need to look at another shelter tomorrow."

Then Oscar and his mom headed home.

As they reached their front door,
Oscar remembered his ball.

When they returned to
the shelter, Mom and Oscar
looked everywhere.

But even with Mrs. Beezley's
help, Oscar's ball could not
be found.

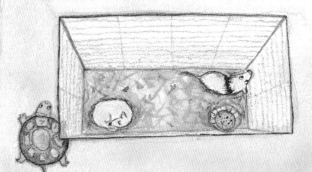
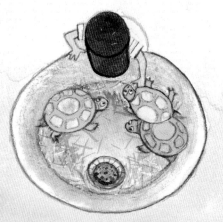

That was because Mr. Beezley had put the ball in the storeroom when he was cleaning up.

But wait . . .

THE BALL!

THE BOY!

What could Broccoli do?

BARK

BARK

BARK!

BARK!

"Just what I wanted!" Oscar exclaimed. "A big, fun dog!"
So Oscar and his mom picked Broccoli as their perfect pet.

Then, as Mrs. Beezley helped Mom and Oscar
adopt Broccoli, something wonderful happened.

Broccoli found his lid.